PHOTOGRAPHY

Written by
John Parsons

HORWITZ
MARTIN
EDUCATION

Contents

Introduction

Surrounded By Photographs

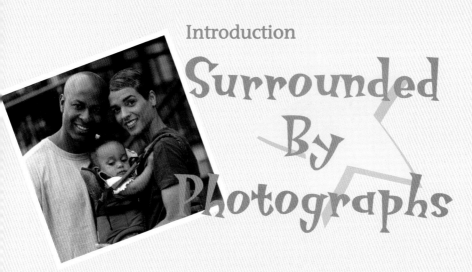

Today we are surrounded by photographs. We can see them almost everywhere. Websites, magazines, books and newspapers are full of photographs of people, places and products. Billboards along roads and highways display huge photographs of things that companies want to sell. And almost every family has at least one photograph album full of holiday snaps.

It is hard to imagine living in a world without photographs to record and display how things look. But a little over 150 years ago, photography hadn't even been invented.

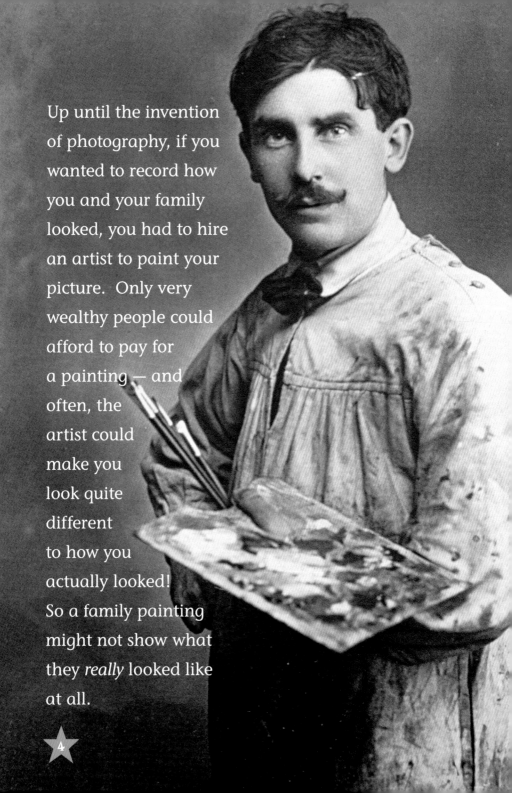

Up until the invention of photography, if you wanted to record how you and your family looked, you had to hire an artist to paint your picture. Only very wealthy people could afford to pay for a painting — and often, the artist could make you look quite different to how you actually looked! So a family painting might not show what they *really* looked like at all.

4

This photograph shows a family from the 1860s. Like many photographs from that time, it is the only record we have of how this family looked and dressed.

Another feature of photography is that you can make as many copies of a photograph as you want. Copies of the old photograph below would have been sent to other family members and friends as a gift.

But in the early days, taking a photograph was not as easy as it is today. A photographer had to learn about light, materials and chemicals. Also, cameras did not work as fast as they do now. The people being photographed would have had to stay still for almost a minute. If they had moved, their photograph would have turned out blurry.

If you try to smile, and stay absolutely still for a whole minute, you'll find out just how hard that is. That's why many photographs of people from the 1800s show them looking very stiff and unsmiling.

In the early days of photography, nobody knew how to make colour photographs. Every photograph was developed in black and white. It was not until the 1930s that colour photography was invented.

Sometimes, black and white photographs were coloured by hand to look more realistic. An artist may have taken hours to create a colour image, using paint and ink.

Chapter 1

Discovering How Cameras Work

The word 'photograph' was invented in 1839. It comes from two Greek words: 'photos', which means 'light'; and 'graphia', which means 'writing'. Together, the two Greek words describe what photography is — writing with light.

The word 'camera' is over 2,000 years older! If the word 'photograph' was invented in 1839, how could we have known about cameras, but not photographs, for so long?

'Camera' is also a Greek word. It means 'a room'. It was first used by Aristotle, an ancient Greek who lived over 2,000 years ago. He discovered something very interesting. If you sit in a dark room which has a tiny hole in one of the walls, light passes through the hole, and an upside-down image of what is outside the room shows up on the opposite wall!

During the early 1500s, artists such as Leonardo da Vinci realised that Aristotle's discovery could help them to draw more accurate pictures of scenery and buildings. First, they would build a special room, with a tiny hole in the wall, next to a scene that they wanted to paint. Then they traced over the image that showed up on the other wall of their room. These rooms were the first cameras — very large cameras!

Using A Camera Room

Outside Scene

Inside Dark Room (Camera)

Image

Tiny hole

The yellow lines show how the light is turned upside down.

Wall of camera room

The 'camera' rooms became popular with many people who liked to just watch, on the wall, what was happening outside. By 1550, artists had started using a small lens in the hole to make the pictures on the wall sharper or more in focus. But even though they were called cameras, artists still recorded the scenes and views by tracing or painting.

A painting

A tracing

Chapter 2

Discovering Photography

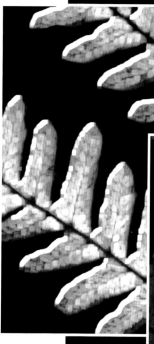

Almost 180 years after camera rooms were used, the next step towards inventing photography was taken. In 1727, a German called Johann Schulze discovered that a chemical called silver nitrate darkened when it was exposed to light.

In the early 1800s, two British scientists, Thomas Wedgwood and Sir Humphrey Davy, coated paper with silver nitrate. They used it to make impressions of leaves and other objects, by placing them onto the paper.

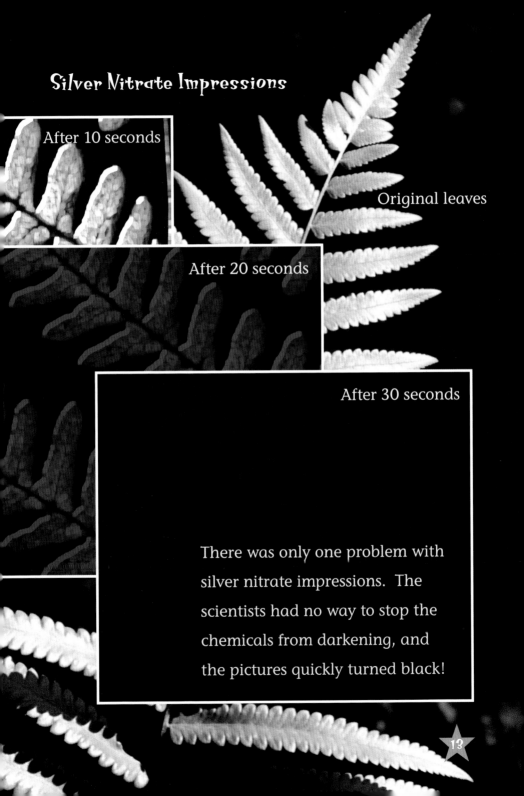

Silver Nitrate Impressions

After 10 seconds

Original leaves

After 20 seconds

After 30 seconds

There was only one problem with silver nitrate impressions. The scientists had no way to stop the chemicals from darkening, and the pictures quickly turned black!

Finally, in 1826, a French chemist named Joseph Niepce worked out how to stop the chemicals from darkening the image. Using a small box with a lens, he took the world's first photograph on a metal plate. It took eight hours to take the photograph!

Niepce realised that this was not very practical, especially when taking photographs of people! He started working with a French artist called Louis Daguerre to discover better chemicals to work with. In 1839, they invented a type of photograph on metal. They called it a daguerreotype. It was quicker to take, clear and did not turn turn black.

An early daguerrotype photograph.

In the same year, an Englishman called William Henry Fox Talbot experimented with another type of photograph. He used chemicals on paper to create a negative, followed by a positive image. Within weeks of the French daguerrotype invention, Fox Talbot announced his discovery.

A negative image

Fox Talbot's invention was much more useful than a daguerreotype, because many copies could be made from a single negative. It is his process of using a negative and a positive that we still use today when we take a photograph. Bad luck for Daguerre and Niepce's process!

A positive image

Chapter 3

Photographic Advances

At the time the photograph on the opposite page was taken, cameras didn't use film. The photographer had to insert a glass plate, covered with chemicals, into the camera.

Every time the photographer wanted to take a new photograph, he or she had to insert a new glass plate into the camera. Used glass plates had to be stored carefully, or else they would shatter and the photograph would be destroyed.

FOTOGRAFIA CESENATE

In the 1860s, photographs had to be processed carefully, too. Sometimes the chemicals that were used to make photographs reacted with other chemicals in the air, or slowly faded when they were exposed to more light. For this reason, many early photographs have now faded. Instead of being black and white, they may be shades of brown, or 'sepia'.

1860

1980

Photo is black and white, and clear.

Photo is brown, and slightly faded.

This is because the chemicals in the photograph are are still reacting. Luckily, we can use photographic technology that has been invented in the last 150 years to make more permanent copies of old photographs, using better chemicals. Without this new technology, many of the old photographs will simply fade and disappear.

Present Day

Photo is pale and faded.

Future

Photo in danger of disappearing.

Chapter 4

Cameras For Everyone

In the mid to late 1800s, many people continued to invent different and better ways to take photographs. But still, they needed to use paper, glass or metal plates coated with chemicals to take their photographs.

Then, in 1885, an American called George Eastman invented a see-through film that could be rolled up and stored inside a camera. Three years later, he invented the Kodak camera. He made up the word 'Kodak' because he thought it would be easy for everyone to remember.

The Kodak camera came loaded with film, and anyone could use it. All people had to do was take their photographs and send the camera *and* film back to Eastman's factory. There, the film would be developed for them. Later, Kodak cameras like the Brownie used film that could be removed and developed.

Suddenly, photography became available to everyone. People bought thousands and thousands of cameras and took millions of photographs. George Eastman became hugely wealthy, and Kodak, the company he started, is still one of the largest photographic companies in the world.

Soon, newspapers, books and magazines
all wanted to publish real photographs,
instead of drawings and paintings of things
in the news. They worked out how to turn a
black and white photograph into a collection
of tiny dots that could then be printed easily
and quickly for their publications.

This picture shows how the photograph on page 26 can be changed into a collection of dots and still be recognised.

Colour Film

In 1930, a Hungarian called Bela Gaspar invented a colour film, which was quickly bought by Eastman's company.

At first, only colour slides could be made but, by 1942, the first film for colour prints became available. The colours were brighter and stronger than those in real life, but people still thought that colour photographs were amazing.

Compare the colours between the original scene (left) and an early colour photograph (right). Which colours have changed the most?

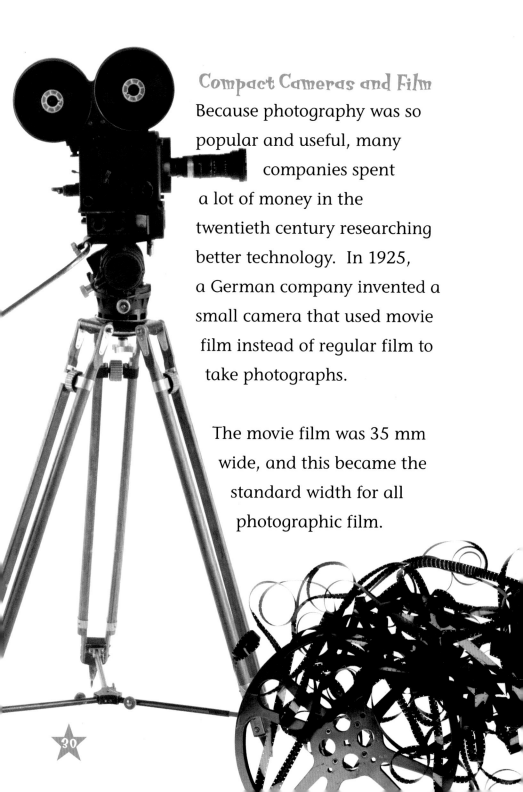

Compact Cameras and Film

Because photography was so popular and useful, many companies spent a lot of money in the twentieth century researching better technology. In 1925, a German company invented a small camera that used movie film instead of regular film to take photographs.

The movie film was 35 mm wide, and this became the standard width for all photographic film.

People preferred to use these smaller cameras, with their smaller films, as they were easier to carry around.

Because of their size, these cameras were called compact cameras. Compact cameras are still very popular today.

A roll of 35 mm film.

Single-Lens Reflex Cameras

In 1936, another German company invented
a type of camera called a single-lens reflex camera.
With this kind of camera, the person taking the
photograph could see exactly what they were taking
a photograph of. Before, people hoped they were
pointing their cameras in the right place!

Inside A Single-Lens Reflex Camera

In a single-lens reflex camera, light passes through the lens (1). Two prisms (2 & 3) bend the light upwards and through the eyepiece (4).

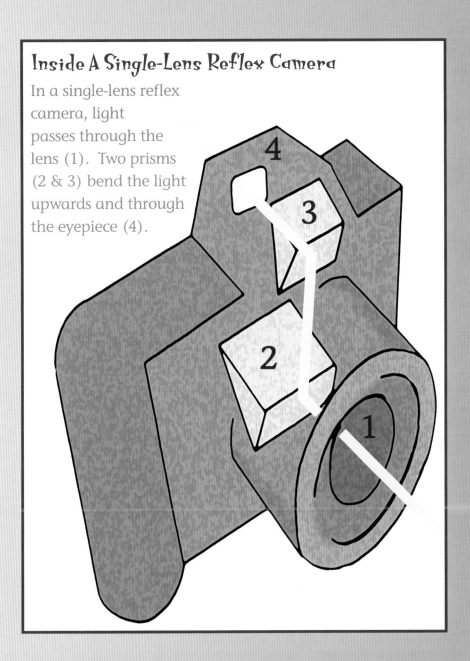

Throughout the twentieth century, films became better and so fast that clear, exciting photographs of speeding objects could be taken. Instead of taking eight hours (as in 1826), cameras can now take photographs in a fraction of a second. Most cameras today can take a good photograph in less than 1/1000th of a second! That's faster than you can blink!

Fast cameras and films allow us to look at details
that our eyes could never capture, like the shape of
a bird flying, a bat hitting a ball, people in mid-air,
and a wave crashing.

Chapter 5

Disposable And Digital Cameras

In the 1990s, disposable cameras were invented. This was a similar idea to when, a little over a hundred years ago, people returned their cameras and film to George Eastman's Kodak company to develop the photographs. Disposable cameras are so cheap that people can use them, and then return them with the film inside for developing. Later, everything in the camera is then recycled into a new product.

Disposable cameras.

In the 1990s, another new type of camera was invented that doesn't even use film. It uses computer technology to store photographs on a disk like a computer disk.

Digital cameras are even more environmentally friendly than film cameras, as they use no chemicals, and produce no waste. Every image that the photographer takes is stored electronically, ready to be printed out using a computer whenever a photograph is required.

A digital photograph can also be easily changed on a computer to remove or change parts of an image. Sometimes, the photograph you see is not a true photograph of what was really there at all!

An even better use for today's photographic technology is that computers can be used to preserve and restore many of the old photographs from the 1800s.

Computers can turn a faded, scratched photo from this ...

While the original photographs may be faded, or torn, or in danger of disappearing altogether, the new technology that has been developed since then enables us to save our precious photographs forever.

A History of Photography

Over 2000 years ago
Aristotle discovers
the properties of
a 'camera'.

1500s
Artists use 'cameras'
to help them draw
and paint scenes.

1839
The word
'photography'
is invented.

1839
Fox Talbot invents a
photographic process
using negatives.

1860s
Glass plates are used
instead of film
in cameras.

1885
Eastman invents
a see-through
photographic film.

1990s
Disposable and
digital cameras
are invented.

1942
First colour
print film
invented.

1727
Schulze discovers the properties of silver nitrate.

Early 1800s
Wedgwood and Davy make silver nitrate impressions on paper.

1839
Niepce and Daguerre invent the daguerrotype.

1826
Niepce takes the first photograph.

1888
Eastman invents the Kodak camera.

1925
Compact cameras, using 35 mm film, are invented.

1936
Single-lens reflex cameras are invented.

1930
Gaspar invents colour slide film.

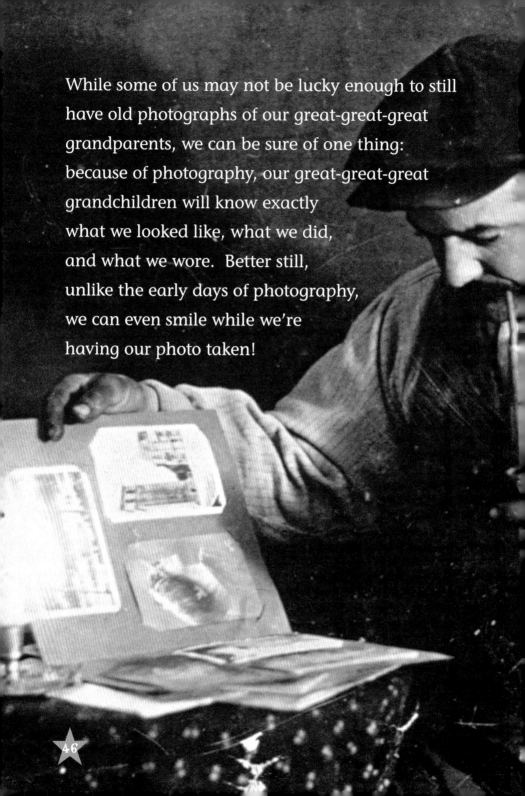

While some of us may not be lucky enough to still have old photographs of our great-great-great grandparents, we can be sure of one thing: because of photography, our great-great-great grandchildren will know exactly what we looked like, what we did, and what we wore. Better still, unlike the early days of photography, we can even smile while we're having our photo taken!

Glossary

Aristotle
A thinker, scientist and teacher born in northern Greece, who lived from 384–322 B.C.

chemicals
Types of substances.

develop
The process of turning film that has been exposed to light into permanent photographs.

disposable
Not able to be used more than once.

exposed
If something is 'exposed' to light, it means that light has been allowed to shine on it.

focus
To get a sharp, clear image.

impressions
Images made from an object.

lens
A curved surface that bends light and allows us to focus clearly.

permanent
Able to be kept forever.

plate
A flat surface or piece of material, such as metal or glass.

preserve
To keep something in good condition.

prism
A triangular-shaped piece of glass that can bend light.

restore
To make something look as good as new.

silver nitrate
A chemical made up of silver, nitrogen and oxygen atoms.

slides
Transparent photographic images which can be projected onto a surface for viewing.

standard
The usual or normal measurement for something, agreed on by most people.

Vinci, Leonardo da
An Italian painter, scientist, inventor and teacher who lived between 1452–1519.

Index